nickelodeon™

ni hao, Kai-lan™

Kai-lan, Princess of Friends

adapted by Veronica Paz
based on the screenplay "Princess Kai-lan" written by Chris Nee and Sascha Paladino
illustrated by Dave Walston

Simon Spotlight/Nickelodeon
New York   London   Toronto   Sydney

Based on the TV series *Ni Hao, Kai-lan!*™ as seen on Nick Jr.™

SIMON SPOTLIGHT/NICKELODEON
An imprint of Simon & Schuster Children's Publishing Division
1230 Avenue of the Americas, New York, New York 10020
For information about special discounts for bulk purchases, please contact Simon & Schuster
Special Sales at 1-866-506-1949 or business@simonandschuster.com.
Manufactured in the United State of America 0710 LAK
First Edition 10 9 8 7 6 5 4 3 2 1
ISBN 978-1-4424-0364-2

Kai-lan and her friends were outside playing Butterfly Ball when their friend the Monkey King appeared.

"Look! It's the Monkey King!" exclaimed Kai-lan. "He can do lots of magical things! He's our favorite superhero!"

"And you're my favorite friends!" replied the Monkey King. "I need your help with a very big problem."

Using his magic stick the Monkey King showed them the Land of Foxes and Bears.

"The Fox Kingdom and the Bear Kingdom are separated by a big wall," the Monkey King told them. "The Foxes and the Bears aren't friends, so they built this wall so they would never, ever have to talk to each other! Kai-lan, you know so much about being a great friend. And you all are such good friends. Will you go with me on an adventure to help the Bears and the Foxes become friends?"

"Of course we'll go with you!" said Kai-lan, Rintoo, Tolee, and Hoho.

The Monkey King gave them special magic robes to help them jump really high. They jumped onto some clouds and floated to the Land of Foxes and Bears.

We're on our way to make new friends today! If you want to make a new friend or two, just find things you both like to do!

"Wow! That wall is so *big*!" roared Rintoo. "How will we get them to be friends if they can't talk to each other?"

"We just need to talk to the Fox King and the Bear Queen," explained Kai-lan.

"This isn't going to be easy, but I know you can do it!" said the Monkey King.

On his way down from the clouds, the Monkey King accidentally crashed into the wall and made a hole in it. He wasn't hurt, but he broke his magic stick and had to go home to fix it. Before he left he told Kai-lan he knew she would find a way to help the Foxes and the Bears and wished her good luck.

"Ooh, look! There's a baby fox," said Kai-lan. "He says his name is Xin Xin."

"*Ni men hao*. I'm happy to meet you!" said Xin Xin.

"Whoa! Who is that on the other side of the wall?" asked Hoho.

"It's a baby bear! Let's all say hi in Chinese—*ni hao!*" exclaimed Kai-lan.

"*Ni hao!*" said the friends excitedly.

"*Ni men hao.* It's good to meet you all! *Wo jiao* Tian Tian! My name is Tian Tian!" replied the baby bear.

Tian Tian saw a peach tree over in the Fox Kingdom. Peaches were his favorite fruit, and he couldn't resist asking Kai-lan for one.

"I don't know, Tian Tian. You'll have to ask Xin Xin for a peach," replied Kai-lan.

"But I've never talked to a fox before!" exclaimed Tian Tian.

"And I've never talked to a bear!" said Xin Xin.

"It's okay—just try it," suggested Kai-lan.

"Um . . . okay. I really love peaches," said Tian Tian shyly.

"Me too! Do you want one?" asked Xin Xin.

"Yeah. Sure! Thank you!" replied Tian Tian. "Do you want to be my friend?"

"Ooh, yes! I *do* want to be your friend!" exclaimed Xin Xin.

"Look! They talked, and now they're friends!" cheered Kai-lan.

Just then some foxes saw the baby bear talking to the baby fox. They told the baby bear to go back to the Bear Kingdom and closed up the wall. The new friends said they would miss each other very much.

"Xin Xin and Tian Tian want to be friends! We have to help them!" said Kai-lan.

"But how?" asked Tolee.

"We need to get the Fox King and the Bear Queen to talk to each other! We can bring peaches for them," said Kai-lan. "First let's go see the Fox King. Tian Tian, will you meet us at the Bear Queen's castle?"

Before they could get to the Fox Castle, the friends came across a magical bamboo forest. Whenever they tried to enter the forest, the magic bamboo made it impossible to pass.

"Hmm . . . we can't go through the bamboo, but maybe we can jump over it using our magic robes," said Kai-lan. "To say 'jump' in Chinese, we say *tiao*!"

"*Tiao! Tiao!*" shouted the friends as they jumped from one bamboo tree to the next.

"We made it through! Super!" said Kai-lan.

When they found the Fox King, he didn't want to talk. Then Kai-lan gave him a peach as a present!

"I do love peaches," said the Fox King. "Well, okay, you can talk for one minute."

"Fox King, a little fox wants to be friends with a little bear," said Kai-lan. "Will you please let them talk to each other?"

"No way! Foxes and Bears can't be friends!" yelled the Fox King. "We're very mad at the Bears! They're always bothering us with their dancing!"

"But how can dancing bother anyone?" asked Hoho.

Suddenly the ground started to rumble and shake.

"What was that?" asked Hoho.

"When the Bears dance, everything shakes!" yelled the Fox King. "We never know when they'll do it or for how long! It makes us so mad. They never think about us at all."

"Did you ever talk to the Bears about how their dancing makes you feel?" asked Kai-lan.

"No," replied the Fox King. "But if the Bear Queen comes to the wall to talk, then I'll come too."

"Super! Let's go talk to the Bear Queen now!" said Kai-lan.

The friends jumped into the air, their magical robes taking them up and up. Soon they arrived in front of the Bear Castle and noticed purple bubbles blocking the bridge to the castle.

"Hmm . . . we can't get past the bubbles, but maybe we can all jump into a bubble and float to the castle," suggested Kai-lan. "To blow the bubble forward, we have to say *chui*!"

"*Chui! Chui!*" shouted the friends.

"We made it! We got across!" cheered Rintoo, Tolee, and Hoho. The baby bear was at the castle waiting for them.

"But wait, bears are guarding the castle. We'll need to put on those guard uniforms to sneak by them!" said Kai-lan, pointing to some uniforms.

"They think we're guards, Kai-lan. It's working!" whispered Hoho.

Kai-lan and her friends walked up to the Bear Queen. She was angry that they had snuck past the guards.

"We're sorry for sneaking past the guards, but we need to talk to you! We even brought you a peach!" Kai-lan said.

"Oh, that's very nice of you. I love peaches," replied the queen. "How may I help you?"

"Bear Queen, a little bear wants to be friends with a little fox," said Kai-lan. "Will you please let them talk to each other?"

"What? Bears and Foxes can't be friends!" yelled the Bear Queen. "We're very mad at the Foxes! They're always bothering us with their singing!"

All of a sudden they heard loud singing.

"No one can hear!" shouted the Bear Queen.

"What?" yelled Rintoo.

"When the Foxes sing, no one can hear, it's so loud! It makes us feel so mad!" said the Bear Queen.

"Wow, that was loud," said Kai-lan after the singing stopped. "But have you ever talked to the Fox King about how the singing makes you feel?"

"No . . . but I guess I can talk to the Fox King," replied the Bear Queen.

"Super!" cheered Kai-lan. "We'll meet you at the wall!"

The Fox King and the Bear Queen finally met at the wall, but they refused to speak to each other. Kai-lan asked them to try.

"I do not talk to the Foxes!" yelled the Bear Queen. "All they do is sing. They never think about us."

"I do not talk to the Bears!" yelled back the Fox King. "We shouldn't have to deal with their dancing!"

"Listen up, everyone! The Bears and the Foxes have been mad at each other for too long!" said Kai-lan. "The Fox King and the Bear Queen really need to talk to each other!"

Then Kai-lan and her friends sang:

When you feel mad, talk about what's making you mad, so your friends can help you, like good friends do!

"Okay, I'll try," said the Fox King. "Bear Queen, I'm mad because when the Bears dance, they make the ground shake so much that the Foxes can't even stand up."

"Oh! I had no idea that was happening. I'm sorry," replied the Bear Queen. "Fox King, I'm mad because when the Foxes sing, it's so loud that the Bears can't talk, or sleep, or think."

"Oh, I'm sorry. I didn't know that was a problem for you," said the Fox King. "You know, I'm glad we're talking about this, but what do we do now?"

"We need to think of a way for the Foxes and the Bears to sing and dance without making each other mad," said Kai-lan. "I know! What if the Foxes sing and the Bears dance once a day at the same time!"

"Okay, let's try it!" cheered the Fox King and the Bear Queen.

The Foxes began singing and the Bears joined in and started to dance in time with the music. Soon both kingdoms were dancing and singing. Everyone was super happy!

"Everyone, I have an announcement—the Bears and the Foxes are finally friends!" cheered Kai-lan.

"Xin Xin, that means we can be friends!" cheered Tian Tian.

"Yay!" shouted Xin Xin.

At that moment the Monkey King appeared and saw the joy and celebration in both kingdoms. He realized it would be hard for them to be friends with that great, big wall in between them. So being the clever Monkey King that he was, he decided to turn the wall into a bridge.

"Hooray! The Foxes and the Bears can visit each other all the time!" said Kai-lan.

"We need a name for our new kingdom . . . since we are all friends now, we should call it the Kingdom of Friends," said the Bear Queen.

"Wonderful! We need one more thing for our kingdom . . . a princess!" said the Fox King.

"Well since Kai-lan knows more than anyone about being a good friend, I think she should be the Princess of Friends," declared the Monkey King.

"Hooray for Kai-lan, Princess of Friends!" cheered the Fox King and the Bear Queen.

"Thank you. As princess, I would like to ask Rintoo, Tolee, and Hoho to be knights of the Kingdom of Friends!" said Kai-lan.

"Yay! We're knights!" cheered her friends. "Thanks, Kai-lan!"

From then on, everyone was happy in the Kingdom of Friends. The Foxes and the Bears danced and sang happily together, but more importantly they learned to talk to each other. With the bridge in place, there would never, ever be a wall between them again.